The Firebird

First published in German under the title *Der Feuervogel*
© 1999 by Bohem Press, Zurich, Switzerland
English version © 1999 Floris Books, 15 Harrison Gardens, Edinburgh
British Library CIP Data available
ISBN 0-86315-302-X
Printed in Italy

The Firebird

A traditional Russian folk-tale
retold by C J Moore

Illustrated by Jindra Capek

Floris Books

Once there lived a King, Berenay by name, who had three sons, and the youngest of them was called Ivan.

The King's palace was surrounded by a garden full of rare flowers and trees which gave him great joy. And of all the precious trees in his garden, he loved a particular apple tree the most, for it bore him golden apples the whole year round.

One summer, he began to notice that apples were missing, two at a time, stolen at night from the tree. He called his guards and ordered them to catch the thief. They mounted a vigil by the tree day and night for a week but saw and heard nothing, and still the golden apples continued to disappear.

Then his eldest son, knowing how much his father loved the golden apple tree, came to him and declared he would catch the thief. That very night, he went out to the garden and slept beneath the tree, his sword in hand. But in the morning he woke to find two apples missing, and swore he had seen and heard nothing.

The second son then went to the king and likewise offered to catch the thief. He sat at the foot of the tree the following night, his sword in hand, determined to stay awake. But in the morning, to his dismay, he found that two more golden apples had been stolen while he nodded, and he too had seen and heard nothing.

Then Ivan, the third and youngest son, came to his father and said he would try to catch the thief. When night fell, he went and kept watch beneath the tree. He took no sword with him.

The hours passed and, as he sat quietly, the darkness around turned suddenly to light and the whole garden filled with a warm glow. There above his head he saw the shining Firebird glide through the air and settle on the tree, where it grasped an apple with each foot. The moment it started to fly away, Ivan leapt up and grabbed its tail. Alarmed, the Firebird flapped its wings to escape and as it rose high into the air, left a gleaming feather in the prince's hand.

Ivan took the feather and went in to the king, saying, "Here, father, this feather belongs to the thief. It is the Firebird which has been stealing your golden apples."

The feather shone in the palace, lighting up the room around them, and all wondered at it. The king, taking the feather in his hand, said he had never seen anything so lovely.

"Whoever will find me this Firebird, I shall reward handsomely," he cried.

Both his elder sons stepped forward and announced that they would go forth and bring back the Firebird for the king. Prince Ivan, too, still dazzled by the shining of the bird, said he would not rest till he had found it.

So early next day the three princes set out from the palace on horseback, and rode off, one to the north, one to the south, and Prince Ivan to the east.

Prince Ivan rode on his way through woods and valleys, enjoying the summer sunshine that warmed his face. After some hours when the midday sun was high in the sky, he stopped to rest and water his horse. Then leaving the animal to graze, he lay down in the shade under a tree and went to sleep.

A while later he woke to hear his horse running off into the woods, startled by a grey wolf which had come close. Ivan leapt to his feet and ran in pursuit but though he wandered far and wide searching for the horse, it was not to be found.

Hot and annoyed, he continued his journey on foot. He walked all that afternoon under the hot sun and became so tired that all he could do was to lie down on the grass.

As he rested, the grey wolf caught up with him and said: "I am sorry, Prince Ivan, that I frightened away your horse and now you are so tired from walking. Tell me where I may carry you and for what purpose."

Ivan explained that he was searching on behalf of his father the king for the shining Firebird which had come to their garden and stolen the apples.

"Come, then, climb on my back," said the wolf, "and I shall take you where the Firebird is to be found. If we go quickly, we can be there by nightfall."

So the prince climbed on the grey wolf's back and the wolf set off as fast as he could through the forest.

As night fell, they came to a high wall where the wolf stopped and said: "In this garden is a stone tower, and in the tower is a cage, and there you will find the Firebird. Take the bird, but be warned! on no account touch the cage."

Prince Ivan climbed over the wall and crept through the garden till he came to the stone tower.

There in the tower hung a golden cage and in the cage shone the Firebird, just as the wolf had said. Carefully Ivan put his hand inside, took hold of the bird, and turned to go. Then he thought how hard it was to carry the bird tucked in his cloak and how easily it might fly away.

"I must have the cage as well," he decided. But the very moment he took the cage down, alarm bells rang all around and as he tried to escape through the garden, guards ran and seized him.

Immediately they took him before their king whose name was Affron. King Affron, furious with the young man, asked who he was and where he was from.

"I am Ivan, third son of King Berenay," the prince answered proudly. "The Firebird has been stealing my father's golden apples, and therefore I promised him I would catch the thief."

"Are you not ashamed, then, to become a thief yourself?" accused the King. "Had you come and told me your story, I should have given you the Firebird with honour."

Prince Ivan looked crestfallen and asked for the King's pardon.

"You may redeem your act by performing a service for me," said King Affron. "Go to the neighbouring kingdom of King Kussman and fetch me the horse with the golden mane. Then I shall give you the Firebird with honour. But if you fail me, I shall have you publicly denounced as a thief."

Ivan went back to the grey wolf and told him everything that had happened.

"Why didn't you listen to what I told you?" the wolf growled gently. "Now I must take you still further, to the land of King Kussman."

The prince mounted the grey wolf's back and they ran and they ran through wood and valley until they came to the walls of King Kussman's palace.

"Here in the royal stables you will find the horse with a golden mane," said the wolf. "Take the horse but, be warned! on no account touch the golden bridle which hangs on the wall."

Prince Ivan crept into the coachyard and made his way to the stables where he found the horse with a golden mane. He took hold of its mane and was turning to go when he saw, glittering on the wall, a beautiful golden bridle.

"How can I lead the horse without a bridle?" he thought, and reaching up, took the golden bridle and placed it round the horse's head.

But he had not taken two steps before the alarm sounded and guards came running. They seized him and took him before King Kussman.

"Who are you?" the King questioned angrily, "and where are you from?"

When Prince Ivan told him his name and his purpose, the King said to him: "You are of royal blood yet you have crept into my stables like a common thief. Are you not ashamed? You must redeem yourself by performing a service for me, or else I must accuse you publicly."

Then he told the prince he had to travel to the very farthest kingdom where lived Princess Vasilissa the Fair.

"I have loved her seven long years and cannot win her for my bride. Fetch her for me and I shall give you the horse with the golden mane and let you go with honour."

Prince Ivan agreed and, going out, went to find the grey wolf and told him all that had happened in the palace.

"Ah, why didn't you listen to me?" the wolf whined quietly. "Now I must carry you still further, to the very farthest kingdom."

The prince mounted the wolf's back and they ran and they ran across mountain and river until in no time at all they came to the farthest kingdom.

"Wait here," said the wolf as they reached the royal grounds. He leapt over the fence and searched until he found Princess Vasilissa walking with her servants.

He quickly jumped out and frightened her so much she ran before him to the spot where Ivan waited and threw herself straight into his arms.

Prince Ivan calmed the princess and told her not to fear. But she, as he held her in his arms, fell instantly in love with him and said she would follow him to the ends of the earth.

They both climbed on the back of the grey wolf who set off with his burden across mountain and valley. They came to a river but with both the princess and the prince on his back he could not leap over as before. Still he plunged without pausing into the flow and the river waters parted to let them through.

In no time at all they came to a hut near the palace of King Kussman and the prince began to weep.

"Whatever is the matter?" asked Vasilissa.

"I am sorrowful because I have promised to give you to King Kussman for his bride," Ivan told here. "But I love you myself with all my heart."

"And I love you, too," responded the princess, and both fell to weeping.

The grey wolf turned to them and said, "I have served you well, Prince Ivan, and I will serve you still. Let me make myself into the image of the princess and you will lead me to the king and claim the horse, as agreed. Then return here to find the princess and wait until I come to you."

With joy the prince fell in with this plan and so leaving the princess safely in the hut, he and the wolf set off for the palace. And in a while the wolf spun around three times and turned into the very likeness of the princess.

When the King saw his bride he was overcome with happiness and straightaway led her to his throne. He gave Prince Ivan the horse with the golden mane and bade him farewell, whereupon Ivan rode off to the hut in the woods to rejoin his beloved.

Meanwhile King Kussman announced a great feast to celebrate his wedding. His princess was led away to be dressed in great finery and that very day they were wed before the whole court.

Inviting the whole land to feast and rejoice, the king accompanied his new bride to the bridal chamber where her servants saw her to bed. Then he came to join her and on pulling back the bedclothes was shocked to find a wolf in her place.

Falling over with fright, the king let out a roar. In an instant, the wolf jumped over his head, leapt right out of the window and ran away as fast as he could.

He found Ivan and Vasilissa waiting in the hut and so they both mounted the horse with the golden mane and all set off on their return to the land of King Affron.

But when the palace came in sight, the prince, filled with sorrow, stopped on the road. He knew that in order to take the Firebird home to his father, he must give up the horse with the golden mane to King Affron. More than anything, though, he wished to arrive home on this fine steed with his beloved.

"Why so sad, my love?" asked the princess. And Ivan explained why he was sorrowful.

Then Prince Ivan said to the wolf, "You have served me well, but could you not serve me one last time?"

The wolf replied: "Yes, I shall serve you once more. Let me make myself into the image of the horse with the golden mane, and you will lead me to King Affron and claim the Firebird, as agreed. Then return here to the princess and wait till I join you."

Joyfully, the prince went with the wolf towards the palace, leaving the horse with the princess. After a moment, the wolf spun round three times and made himself into the very likeness of the horse.

So they came into the presence of King Affron who was highly delighted to receive the horse with the golden mane. He gave Ivan the Firebird in its cage and bade him farewell. Whereupon the prince quickly made his way back to the princess.

That very afternoon, the king wished to enjoy a ride on his new steed, so he saddled and mounted it and rode out through his lands. But when he reached the open and spurred it on, the horse beneath him turned into a wolf and ran off, throwing the king to the ground.

Meanwhile, Prince Ivan rode towards home with his princess, the horse with the golden mane and the Firebird in its cage.

The grey wolf, catching up with them, said, "This is the very spot where I frightened away your horse. I have served you and made amends, so now I bid you farewell."

The prince thanked the wolf and said farewell, and they parted sadly.

Just then the prince's brothers happened to pass, returning empty-handed from their journeys. On seeing their younger brother with the Firebird, the horse and the beautiful princess, they were filled with jealousy and taking him by surprise they killed him and left him lying on the ground, dividing the spoils between them.

Soon a raven settled by the body and called others to come. Hearing the commotion, the grey wolf hastened back and found the prince lying dead. He seized the raven and threatened to kill it. But he would spare its life, he said, if it fetched for him the water of death and the water of life from the kingdom beyond the farthest kingdom.

The raven flew off and in no time at all returned with the water of death and the water of life. These the wolf sprinkled in turn on the body of the dead prince and watched as the young man stirred once again, opened his eyes and sat up.

Quickly, Ivan mounted the wolf's back and they raced after his brothers to claim back the princess, the horse and the Firebird. And when they caught up with them on the road, the wolf leapt angrily upon the villains and devoured the two of them there and then to punish them for their treachery.

Prince Ivan embraced Vasilissa with joy and comforted her. They could barely thank the wolf enough for helping them yet again.

"I have served you well, and my service is now done," he said, and padded away into the forest.

So it was that Prince Ivan came home bearing the Fire-bird in its cage. He rode proudly on the horse with the golden mane, with Princess Vasilissa the Fair before him.

Vasilissa told King Berenay how Ivan's brothers had betrayed him and the price they had paid for their deed. Then the King greeted his youngest son and made him the heir to his kingdom, calling on all to celebrate his safe return.

Prince Ivan soon married Vasilissa and on the death of his father they lived and ruled in friendship and love for the rest of their days.

The Star-Child

A fable by Oscar Wilde
Illustrated by Jindra Capek

A star falls from the winter sky into a wood, and there two shepherds find a strange infant. One of them takes the baby home and raises it as his own.

Though exquisitely beautiful of face and form, the Star-Child turns out to be a cruel and selfish boy. One day he taunts a poor beggar-woman who, to his horror, then claims to be his mother. He rejects her and from that moment, his beauty forsakes him and he becomes an outcast, despised and shunned for his ugliness.

Oscar Wilde's powerful and moving fable of beauty and evil is dramatically illustrated by the Czech artist, Jindra Capek.

Floris Books